W9-CAI-693

This book belongs to:

_____

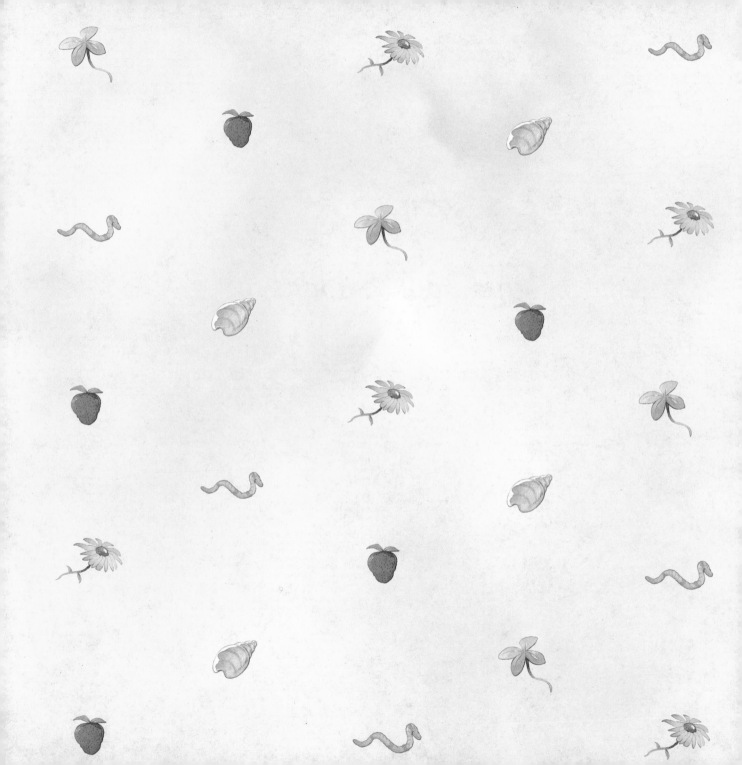

Five Little Ducks

for Thomas and Anna

ISBN-13: 978-0-439-92407-8
ISBN-10: 0-439-92407-3

Copyright © 2006 by Ivan Bates. All rights reserved. Published by Orchard Books,
an imprint of Scholastic Inc. ORCHARD BOOKS and design are registered trademarks
of Watts Publishing Group, Ltd., used under license. SCHOLASTIC and associated logos
are trademarks and/or registered trademarks of Scholastic Inc.

12 11 10 9 8 7 6 5 4   11 12 13 14 15/0
Printed in the U.S.A.   40
First Scholastic paperback printing, June 2007

The illustrations for this book were done in colored pencil and watercolor on Arches paper.
The text type was set in Poliphilus MT Regular.
The display type was set in Script MT.
Book design by Alison Klapthor

Five Little Ducks

Illustrated by IVAN BATES

SCHOLASTIC INC.

New York   Toronto   London   Auckland   Sydney
Mexico City   New Delhi   Hong Kong   Buenos Aires

Five little ducks
Went out one day
Over the hills and far away.
Mother duck said,
"Quack, quack, quack."

But only four little ducks
came waddling back.

Four little ducks
Went out one day
Over the hills and far away.
Mother duck said,
"Quack, quack, quack."

But only three little ducks
came waddling back.

Three little ducks
Went out one day
Over the hills and far away.
Mother duck said,
"Quack, quack, quack."

But only two little ducks
came waddling back.

Two little ducks
Went out one day
Over the hills and far away.
Mother duck said,
"Quack, quack, quack."

But only one little duck
came waddling back.

One little duck
Went out one day
Over the hills and far away.
Mother duck said,
"Quack, quack, quack."

But no little ducks
came waddling back.

Sad mother duck
Went out one day
Over the hills and far away.
Mother duck cried,
"Quack, quack, quack."

And all five little ducks
came waddling back!

Five Little Ducks

Brightly

Repeat melody for each verse

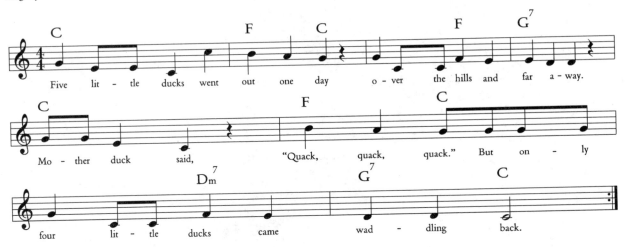

Five lit – tle ducks went out one day o – ver the hills and far a – way.

Mo – ther duck said, "Quack, quack, quack." But on – ly

four lit – tle ducks came wad – dling back.

Verse 2	Verse 3	Verse 4	Verse 5	Verse 6
Four little ducks	Three little ducks	Two little ducks	One little duck	Sad mother duck
Went out one day	Went out one day	Went out one day	Went out one day	Went out one day
Over the hills and far away.	Over the hills and far away.	Over the hills and far away.	Over the hills and far away.	Over the hills and far away.
Mother duck said,	Mother duck said,	Mother duck said,	Mother duck said,	Mother duck cried,
"Quack, quack, quack."	"Quack, quack, quack."	"Quack, quack, quack."	"Quack, quack, quack."	"Quack, quack, quack."
But only three little ducks	But only two little ducks	But only one little duck	But no little ducks	And all five little ducks
came waddling back.	came waddling back.	came waddling back.	came waddling back.	came waddling back!